Party Time!

Want to know the secrets to a *purrr*-fect party? You've come to the right place! The Littlest Pet Shop pets have tons of tips, activities, crafts, and recipes to help you plan a super party. Let's go!

Party #1 Tip

Have a gift bag for each guest with her name on the front. As you create different crafts, have each friend place her finished projects in the bag. At the end of the party, she'll be able to take the bag home with her!

Sensational Invitations

The first step to planning a party is to send an invitation. Try designing your own or try something like this:

 Come to my party!

Date: _____

Place: _____

Drop-off time: _____

Pickup time: _____

Party #2 Tip

Send your invitations in the mail, deliver them in person, or send an e-mail. But whatever you do, be sure to give your friends plenty of advance notice so they can save the date!

SCHOLASTIC INC.
New York Toronto London Auckland Sydney
Mexico City New Delhi Hong Kong Buenos Aires

- ADOPTION CERTIFICATE -

This certifies that

_____

(your name here)

adopted _____

(your pig's name here)

_____

Date

ISBN-13: 978-0-545-03425-8
ISBN-10: 0-545-03425-6

LITTLEST PET SHOP is a trademark of Hasbro and is used with permission.
© 2007 Hasbro. All Rights Reserved.

Published by Scholastic Inc. SCHOLASTIC and associated logos are trademarks and/or registered trademarks of Scholastic Inc.

12 11 10 9 8 7 6 5 4 3 2 1   8 9 10 11 12/0

Printed in China
First printing, August 2008

Party #3 Tip

Check out the recipes and crafts in this book and decide which ones you'd like to make at your party. Then take a look around the house and make a list of all the things you'll need that you already have. Use that list to determine what you still need, and either assign different items to your friends or use the list below to keep track of the items you'll have to get before the party.

Things I Have

_____

_____

_____

_____

_____

_____

_____

_____

_____

_____

_____

Things I Need

_____

_____

_____

_____

_____

_____

_____

_____

_____

_____

_____

Yoga Party!

Host a yoga party and try these simple poses with your friends! Remember: Yoga isn't supposed to hurt. If you feel pain at any time, stop right away.

Funky Monkey Stretch

1) Begin in a kneeling position.

2) Put your right leg straight out in front of you.

3) Slowly slide the right heel forward as far as you can, so that you are doing a split.

4) Lace your fingers together, push your palms out in front of you, and then raise your arms over your head while arching your back.

5) Hold the pose for 5–10 breaths and then repeat with your left leg.

Party #4 Tip

Yoga is easiest to do with bare feet! It's also a good idea to wear loose, comfortable clothing.

4

Funny Bunny Pose

1) Begin on your hands and knees.
2) Place the top of your head on the floor between your hands.
3) Lift your feet off the floor so that you are balancing on your knees.
4) Reach back and grab your ankles.
5) Hold the pose for 5–10 breaths and then return to your beginning position.

Fish Out of Water

1) Sit on your hands, with your palms pressed down against the floor.
2) Lie on your back with your legs straight.
3) Push your hands and arms against the floor, and lift your chest, arching your back.
4) Touch the top of your head to the ground without putting a lot of weight on it.
5) Hold the pose for 5–10 breaths and then return to your beginning position.

Puppy Pose

1) Begin on your hands and knees.
2) Pushing off the balls of your feet, lift your hips and straighten your legs.
3) Hang your head down between your arms, and hold the position for 5–10 breaths.
4) Slowly relax and then return to your beginning position.

Autograph Book

This is a great craft to do with friends. Make sure you have enough materials so you can each make your own book. Then you can trade books and write each of your friends a special autograph and note!

What you'll need for each book:

- *3 blank sheets of 8 1/2 x 11 paper*
- *1 sheet colored paper*
- *hole punch*
- *ribbon or yarn*

- *digital camera*
- *color printer*
- *glue*
- *stickers, buttons, construction paper, and other craft materials*

BEST FRIENDS FOREVER!

What you'll do:

1) Fold the 3 sheets of 8 1/2 x 11 paper in half horizontally. This is the inside of your 12-page book.

2) Next create a book cover by folding the colored paper around the 3 sheets you folded in step 1. Be sure to line up the book cover with the interior pages.

3) Punch two holes in the spine of the book.

4) Take a pretty piece of yarn or some ribbon, thread it through the holes, and tie the string together.

5) Take a photo of yourself with your friends and print out a few copies on a color printer. You can each glue this picture to the front cover of your book.

6) Decorate your books with stickers, buttons, markers, and other photos.

7) Write your name on the first page of the book. The other pages will be for your friends' autographs.

8) Finally, set the book aside to dry overnight. The next morning, autograph one another's books while eating breakfast. Everyone will have an unforgettable party favor to take home!

Dance Contest!

Break into teams of two and pick your favorite song. Take 30 minutes to choreograph a dance routine with your partner and then perform for your friends. After everyone has performed, vote via secret ballot for your favorite dance routine!

Party #5 Tip

Try one of these animal-themed songs: "Who Let the Dogs Out?," "Crocodile Rock," or "Rockin' Robin"!

Game Time!

What you'll need:

- *Different animal pictures clipped from magazines. You should have one picture for each person.*
- *Tape*

What you'll do:

Place all of the animal pictures facedown on a table. Each player should select a photo and use a piece of tape to stick it to a friend's back. Don't let your friend see what type of animal she is! The goal is to figure out what animal you are based on the way the other players talk to you. You can give your friends hints, too!

Concession Stand

No party is complete without snacks! Try one or more of these fun and delicious treats.

Pigs in a Blanket

What you'll need:

- Mini hot dogs
- Prepackaged crescent rolls
- Ketchup, mustard, and barbecue sauce

What you'll do:

First ask an adult for help. Open the package of crescent rolls and separate the dough along the dotted lines. Place one hot dog along the longest part of the dough. Roll the hot dog in the dough. Place on a baking sheet that has been sprayed with cooking spray. Repeat until all of the dough has been used. Follow the baking instructions on the package. Serve with different condiments.

Hamster Veggie Platter

What you'll need:

- *A variety of precut veggies*
- *Two different salad dressings*

What you'll do:

Pour the salad dressings into two bowls and place a spoon in each. Place the salad dressings in the middle of a platter. Arrange your favorite small veggies around the dips and get ready to nibble!

Bird Food

What you'll need:

- *Three cups of granola*
- *Two cups of toasted whole or sliced almonds*
- *One cup of sunflower seeds*
- *Half a package of your favorite cereal*
- *One bag of golden raisins*

What you'll do:

Pour all ingredients into a large bowl and mix with a spoon. Serves 8 friends.

Marshmallow Cereal Treats

What you'll need:

- 3 tablespoons butter
- One 10-oz. package marshmallows
- Six cups of puffed rice cereal

What you'll do:

In a large microwave-safe bowl, heat butter and marshmallows for three minutes. Halfway through the cooking time, stop and stir the ingredients. After ingredients are melted, remove from microwave and add the puffed rice cereal. Once completely mixed, use a spatula to spread the mixture into a 9 x 13 pan that is coated with cooking spray. Let mixture cool before cutting.

Try this!

Dog Biscuits

Use a dog-bone-shaped cookie cutter (or any other shaped cookie cutter) to carefully cut out shaped marshmallow cereal treats. Arrange them in a new, clean, dog bowl to serve!

Cheese Platter and Crackers

What you'll need:

- *Three different kinds of cheese*
- *Three types of crackers*

What you'll do:

First ask an adult for help. Carefully slice the three cheeses. Arrange the first type of cheese beginning in the center of the plate and work your way out to the edge of the plate. Then arrange the first type of crackers in the same way next to the first type of cheese. Repeat again with the next cheese and the next kind of cracker. Continue alternating until you have filled the plate.

Monkey Bread

What you'll need:

- 1 1/2 cups flour
- 3 ripe bananas, mashed
- 1 teaspoon salt
- 1 teaspoon vanilla
- 1 teaspoon baking soda
- 1/3 cup melted butter
- 1 cup sugar
- 1 egg, beaten

What you'll do:

First ask an adult for help. Then preheat the oven to 350°F. Next mix the butter and mashed bananas in a large bowl. Add the sugar, egg, and vanilla and mix well. Stir in baking soda, salt, and flour. Butter a 4 x 8 bread loaf pan. Pour the mixture into the pan and bake for 60 minutes, or until the bread is done. You can check by inserting a toothpick into the middle of the bread—if it comes out clean, it's ready! Just remove the pan from the oven, let it cool, and remove the bread from the pan. Slice and serve!

Party #6 Tip

Serve the bread with cream cheese or butter and a side of fruit. It's the perfect treat for a brunch or lunchtime party.

Spa Party!

Invite your friends over for an afternoon of pampering! First make the bubble bath and lip gloss. Your friends can take these home as party favors. Then treat yourselves to fun froggy facials!

Bunny Bubble Bath

Mix one cup of your favorite fruity shampoo, half a cup of unscented liquid soap, and three tablespoons of water in a resealable plastic bag. Squish the contents together with your hands. Squeeze all of the contents of the bag into one bottom corner of the bag. Clip off the corner of the bag and carefully squeeze the mixture into a medium-size container or bottle. If you like, use stickers to decorate the outside of the bottle.

Fish Lip Gloss

Place three tablespoons of petroleum jelly and one tablespoon of your favorite flavored sugar-free powdered drink mix in a resealable plastic bag. Seal the bag and place it in a bowl of very warm water for 4 minutes. Remove the bag and squish the jelly and flavoring with your hands until mixed. Squeeze all of the contents of the bag into one bottom corner of the bag. Clip off the corner of the bag and carefully squeeze the mixture into a small container. Refrigerate for several hours until set. Apply to lips using your fingertips.

Froggy Facial

Try this moisturizing face mask. Mash an avocado in a small bowl. Use your hands to spread evenly over your face, being careful to avoid your eyes. Leave it on for 15 to 20 minutes. Gently rinse the mask off with cool water and a soft washcloth.

Game Time!

Play pet su doku with your friends!

What you'll do:
Fill in the empty boxes, making sure you don't repeat a letter in any row going across the grid, in any column going up and down, or in the 2 x 2 grid within the larger grid. The four letters used in each puzzle spell out the name of the pet shown.

Easiest Puzzle

R			G
O		F	R
G	O		F
F		G	O

Harder Puzzle

B	D		I
	R		
		B	
R		I	D

Hardest Puzzle

	I		S
	F		H
	H		
	S		I

Party #7 Tip

Use a pencil in case you make a mistake!

Recycled Greeting Cards

This is a fun craft to do with your friends. You can recycle old greeting cards into fabulous new ones!

What you'll need:

- construction paper
- feathers
- buttons
- yarn
- colored markers
- wrapping paper
- magazines
- stickers
- used greeting cards

What you'll do:

Use plain white paper, magazine images, wrapping paper, or photos to make a collage over the parts of the card that you'd like to redesign. You can cover up the card's original message so you can write your own, or you can choose to reuse the message. Try some of the cute pet sayings on the next page, or come up with your own!

PUPPY LOVE

YOU'RE PURRR-FECT

BIRDS OF A
FEATHER STICK
TOGETHER

SLOW AND STEADY
WINS THE RACE

SOME BUNNY LOVES YOU

COOL CAT

HUGS AND FISHES

BEE MINE

Pet Purse

What you'll need:

- One 24-inch length of colored ribbon
- One 7 x 14-inch piece of animal print fabric
- Buttons or fabric scraps for decoration
- Pins
- Needle
- Thread

What you'll do:

First ask an adult for help. Turn the fabric inside out and fold in half to create a 7 x 7-inch square. Pin the sides of the purse together. This will keep the fabric stable when sewing. Carefully sew up the sides of the square, leaving the top portion open. Then turn the pouch right side out so that you can now see the pattern. Next pin the ribbon to the inside edge of the fabric on the left side of the purse. Decide how long you want the handle to be, and pin the other end of the ribbon to the inside edge of the fabric on the right side. Carefully sew the ribbon to the bag, being careful to only sew the ribbon to the one side of the bag and not all the way through. Repeat this step on the other side of the purse. If you like, sew on buttons or fabric scraps for decoration.

Party #8 Tip

If you want to do this craft with some friends, make sure you have enough materials for everyone!

DOG TAG JEWELRY

What you'll need:

- *colored string or cord*
- *poster board*
- *silver paint*
- *hole punch*
- *metallic gel pens*
- *large beads*

What you'll do:

Using the template provided, trace two dog tags on the poster board. Then cut out the tags. Next paint one side of the paper silver. Once dry, turn over the dog tags and paint the other side silver as well. When both sides are dry, punch a hole on the right side of both tags. Use the gel pens to write your name, your friends' names, or your pet's name on the tags. Carefully run the colored string or cord through the holes. Finally, add colored beads to each side of the string and tie around your neck.

YOUR DOG TAG TEMPLATE

Purr That Tune

In teams of 2 to 3 people, hum your favorite songs. The team that guesses the song correctly wins a point. The team that reaches 10 points first wins!

Sleepover Fun!

Sleepovers are a great idea for a party. Try solving this sleepover-themed crossword on your own or with a friend!

Across

2. What a frog says
4. An animal that barks
5. Littlest _____ Shop
7. A warm pie that's covered in cheese
8. These keep your feet warm
9. What a cat says
10. _____ out of water
11. A party that requires a sleeping bag and pillow

Down

1. Stay up past _____
3. Sleeping _____
5. A soft place to rest your head
6. A meal served in the morning
7. Abbreviation for pajamas
10. Best _____

22

Can you find the sleepover-themed words listed below?
The words may read forward, backward, up, down, or diagonally.
Bonus: Can you find the word "pet" hidden three different times?

PILLOW	MIDNIGHT
SLEEPING BAG	BREAKFAST
PAJAMAS	SLIPPERS
DANCING	POPCORN
FRIENDS	PIZZA
EYE MASK	GAMES
ROBE	CHARADES
MOVIES	

```
S E D A R A H C V M C R I G L
T Q C P R B M O V I E S P A N
T E P B M I D N I G H T P M M
W T I H B J R A F P W N S E T
S S R O B E A I N O N A Y S X
L Z L F X Y I R L C Z L A B S
E D F I S K O L P Z I F J G D
E P O G P C I I I M K N Z L N
P G Q G P P E P G A V W G S E
I H B O Y X E Y E U D R T R I
N B P U S B C R E R G E A V R
G J H Z O R B K S M P Y D T F
B U P O E W S X J K A I C V E
A K E L P A J A M A S S C P D
G F T Q Q E U X F V M I K M N
```

Pretty Pet Pillowcase

What you'll need:

- an old white pillowcase
- fabric markers
- computer
- color printer
- iron-on printer paper
- iron

What you'll do:

This is a great sleepover party craft. First ask an adult for help. Print out a picture of your favorite pet or animal on the iron-on printer paper. You can use a digital photo of your own pet if you like. Have an adult help you iron the image onto your pillowcase. With the fabric markers, decorate your pillowcase around the iron-on image. Let your pillowcase dry overnight before using.

Party Tip #9

You can iron an image onto a plain, solid-colored T-shirt instead of a pillowcase if you prefer!

24

Rise & Shine!

The morning after your sleepover party, serve your guests monkey bread for breakfast (see page 13 for recipe), or serve any extra bird food with milk for a delicious granola breakfast cereal! Add sliced strawberries on top for a real treat.

While you and your friends are having breakfast, pass your autograph books around (see page 6 for craft directions). Ask your friends to write about their favorite part of the party or leave you a message about why you're a great friend.

Activity Answers

Pages 16-17

R	F	O	G
O	G	F	R
G	O	R	F
F	R	G	O

B	D	R	I
I	R	D	B
D	I	B	R
R	B	I	D

H	I	F	S
S	F	I	H
I	H	S	F
F	S	H	I

Page 22

Across / Down crossword:

1. M — MIDNIGHT (down)
2. RIB
3. BET — BAG (down)
4. DOG
5. PET
6. B — BREAKFAST (down)
7. PIZZA — J... (down)
8. SLIPPERS
9. MEOW
10. FISH — FRIENDS (down)
11. SLEEPOVER

Page 23

Word search:

```
S E D A R A H C V M C R I G L N
T Q C P R B M O V I E S P M E M
T E P B M I D N I G H T H A M T
W T I H B J R A F P W N S E S X
S S R O B E A I N O N A Y S S D
L Z L F X Y I R L C Z L A B S N
E D F I S K O L P Z I F J G D
E P O G P P E P G A V W G S
P G Q Q P P E Y E U D R T N
I H B O Y X E Y E U D R T I
N B P U S B C R E R G E A V E
G J H Z O R B K S M P Y D T F
B U K P O E W S X J K A I C V E
A K E L P A J A M A S S C P D
G F T Q Q E U X F V M I K M N
```